For Amberly

First U.S. edition 2017

Library of Congress Catalog Card Number pending
ISBN 978-0-7636-9296-4

16 17 18 19 20 21 TWP 10 9 8 7 6 5 4 3 2 1

Printed in Johor Bahru, Malaysia

This book was typeset in Times New Roman.
The illustrations were done in ink and watercolor.

TEMPLAR BOOKS

an imprint of
Candlewick Press
99 Dover Street
Somerville, Massachusetts 02144
www.candlewick.com

Sam Usher

RAIN

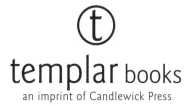

templar books
an imprint of Candlewick Press

When I woke up this
morning, it was raining.

I couldn't wait to
get outside.

Granddad said perhaps
it was best to stay
indoors, but I said
I liked going out in
the rain.

You can catch raindrops,

splash in puddles,

and look at everything
upside down.

But Granddad said . . .

"Let's wait for the rain to stop."

So we waited . . .

and waited.

But did the rain stop?

No.

So I said, "Granddad, I'd like to go on
a voyage with sea monsters."

And Granddad said, "Let's just wait
for the rain to stop."

But did the rain stop?

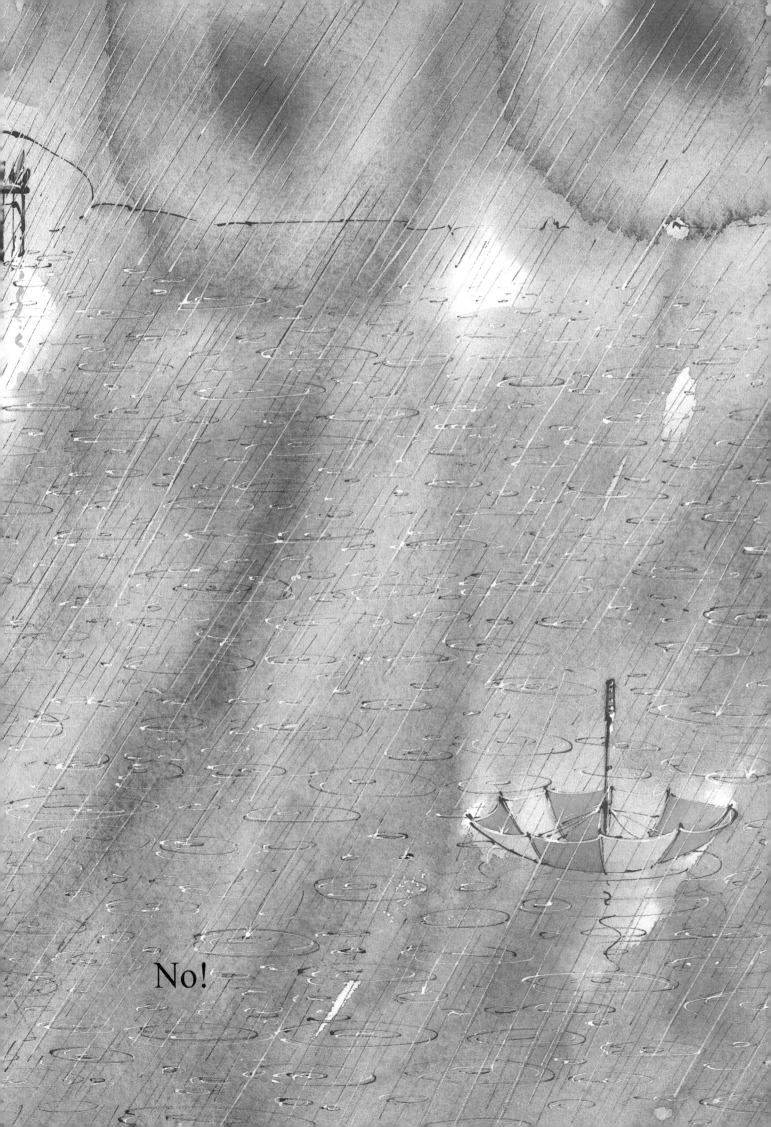

No!

So we waited some more.

And Granddad got
very busy writing.

I said, "Granddad,
I'd like to visit the floating city . . .

with acrobats and carnivals and
musical boatmen!"

And Granddad said . . .

"Quick! Let's go—I need to get this in the mail!"

But had the rain stopped?

YES!

There wasn't a moment to lose.

So we got ready . . .

and stepped outside.

It was time for an adventure at last.

Granddad made me captain.

It started to rain again . . .

so we caught raindrops.

And Granddad let me mail
his important letter.

Back on dry land,
with warm socks
and hot chocolate,
Granddad said,
"You see, the
very best things
are always worth
waiting for."

And I agreed.

I hope it rains
again tomorrow.